RISING★STARS

ISBN: 9781398325562

Text © Steve Cole
Illustrations, design and layout © Hodder and Stoughton Ltd
First published in 2022 by Hodder & Stoughton Limited (for its Rising Stars imprint, part of the Hodder Education Group),
An Hachette UK Company
Carmelite House, 50 Victoria Embankment, London EC4Y 0DZ
www.risingstars-uk.com

Impression number 10 9 8 7 6 5 4 3 2 1
Year 2026 2025 2024 2023 2022

Author: Steve Cole
Series Editor: Tony Bradman
Commissioning Editor: Hamish Baxter
Illustrator: Miriam Serafin/Advocate Art
Educational Reviewer: Helen Marron
Design concept: Gary Kilpatrick
Page layouts: Rocket Design (East Anglia) Ltd
Editor: Amy Tyrer

With thanks to the schools that took part in the development of *Reading Planet* KS2, including: Ancaster CE Primary School, Ancaster; Downsway Primary School, Reading; Ferry Lane Primary School, London; Foxborough Primary School, Slough; Griffin Park Primary School, Blackburn; St Barnabas CE First & Middle School, Pershore; Tranmoor Primary School, Doncaster; and Wilton CE Primary School, Wilton.

A catalogue record for this title is available from the British Library.

Printed in the UK.

Orders: Please contact Hachette UK Distribution, Hely Hutchinson Centre, Milton Road, Didcot, Oxfordshire, OX11 7HH.

Telephone: (44) 01235 400555. Email: primary@hachette.co.uk.

Contents

The story so far

By Ana Pirelli, aged 10

My brother, Rocco, and I were accidentally picked up by a time-travelling coach from the year 3000!

The coach is owned by Time Tours, and they really live up to their name. They took us back to the year 1838 to see Queen Victoria's coronation! But the coach broke down and had to be taken back ... without us!

Rocco and I were busy helping a boy from the future called Ifan. He'd been mistaken for a thief and was put in jail!

We got him out and dealt with the real crook, too – with some help from Tori, the Time Tours robot tour guide.

With the coach out of order, Time Tours sent a time pod to pick us up. It's like a lifeboat for time travellers!

Rocco, Ifan and I begged Tori to take us on another trip through time before we went back home. After all, what could go wrong ...?

"So! Where do you want to go?" said Tori in her squeaky voice. "I love giving Time Tours guests a tour through time!" She was a silver robot in a shiny blue uniform with a small satellite dish on her head.

"Hmm, I'm not sure," said Rocco.

"It's hard to decide," said Ana.

"Anywhere sunny with loads of space," said Ifan dreamily. "When I go back home, I'll be playing virtual football and going to virtual school and stuck in my teeny-tiny bedroom for weeks!"

Ana and Rocco both felt sorry for Ifan. They'd learned that by the year 3000 there was hardly any space left on Earth. That was why Time Tours gave people holidays in olden times, where there were fewer people on the planet and much more room.

"Yes, let's do what Ifan wants," said Ana. "We're already wearing our wonder-onesies – we'll fit in wherever we go."

Rocco nodded. Tori had given them these 'smart clothes' from the future. Wonder-onesies were voice-activated and looked like white plastic overalls with a built-in shower cap, but they could dress you correctly for any time in history.

"I know where I'll take you!" said Tori.

"Where?" asked Rocco.

"It's a surprise," said Tori. She worked the time pod's controls with her mechanical fingers. Shutters slid down over the windows and the engines throbbed with power. "Stand by! Entering the time-flow … now!"

The time pod shot away like a rollercoaster. Patterns of light blazed past the windscreen. Rocco and Ana clung on to each other and Ifan whooped with excitement.

Then Ana saw something dark tumbling towards them. "What's that?"

"Look out!" cried Tori.

There was a shuddering crash. The lights flashed and dimmed. Rocco, Ifan and Ana were thrown forwards into Tori. They knocked her into the controls and sparks shot out.

"What did we hit?" yelled Ifan.

"I don't know," said Tori. "But we're out of control!"

The time pod spun and flipped like a panicking pigeon. Airbags burst from the floor and ceiling to hold everyone in place until the time pod came to a shaking stop. Then the airbags were sucked back into the walls.

"You said you'd give us a surprise, Tori," said Rocco weakly. "Well, you did!"

"On behalf of Time Tours, I apologise for that emergency landing," said Tori.

"It wasn't your fault," said Ana kindly.

"Where are we?" asked Rocco.

"I don't know," said Tori. "I was going to take you on a tour of prehistoric times – there was so much space back then! But whatever we hit has knocked us off course." She checked a flickering screen. "We seem to have landed in Mexico in the sixth century. In the city of Teotihuacan."

"Where?" asked all three children together.

"Tee-oh-tee-wah-karn," said Tori more slowly. "It is a special word meaning 'birthplace of the gods'."

"What a tongue-twister," said Ana.

"Oh dear," said Tori, still studying her screen. "The time pod is so badly damaged, the fuel rods are cracked. There is a chance they could explode!"

"We'd better get out then!" said Ifan.

Tori forced the door open with her robot hands. Outside, all was in darkness. The air was cold and musty. Water dripped from a low, rocky roof.

"Doesn't look much like Mexico to me!" said Rocco. He stepped outside nervously. "It's some kind of cave."

Ana joined him. "At least there's no one about to see the time pod," she said. "Hey, look!" She pointed to a squashed black box with red wires sticking out from the front. "That must be what we hit."

Ifan pulled it free as Tori came to see. "It looks like a drive unit from an early time-travel machine," she said. "Perhaps there was an accident and it came off."

"And it's been floating about in-between times ever since," Ifan added. "Waiting for someone to crash into it!"

"Can you fix the time pod, Tori?" asked Rocco.

"I will need tools," said Tori, tucking the squashed drive unit into her jacket pocket. "They will be hard to find here in this time."

Ana thought back to her history lessons. "Was Teotihuacan built by the Mayans?"

"Scanning memory banks," said Tori, and her satellite dish spun about. "The Mayans were only one group living in Mexico at this time. There were many others. No one knows who built Teotihuacan – only how the city came to an end. It was attacked and left deserted at the end of the sixth century."

"So, any time now then!" said Rocco.

"What a great place to find ourselves stuck!" said Ifan. "Can't you ask Time Tours for help?"

Tori shook her head. "The communicator is as broken as everything else!"

"We'll just have to leave this smelly old cave and ask someone here for help," said Ana.

"Wait," said Rocco. "We don't speak the language."

"Don't worry about that," said Tori. "As tour guide, I can give you instant voice-to-brain translation wherever I am – so long as I have some power left."

Rocco was impressed. "You're a pretty cool invention, Tori. What else can you do?"

"I can shine light on any subject," she said as torch beams came out of her eyes! But as the light spread through the cave, everyone gasped. Strange stone statues of deer and jaguars were sticking up from the sandy ground. A doorway had been carved into the rock ahead of them.

"This isn't just a cave," Ana whispered. "It's some kind of room."

"It's creepy," said Ifan nervously. "I hope that door leads outside."

Rocco and Ana put their weight against the door. It slid slowly open into another small dark chamber. Tori's torchlight showed a skeleton lying on a block of stone. The skeleton was surrounded by strange objects: a conch-shell ink pot, a bone with writing on it, a bead-and-feather necklace, ornaments carved from green stone, knives made of rock ...

"These things are signs of wealth and power," Tori said. "This is a burial chamber for someone important – like a pharaoh's tomb."

"I wish I could take a picture," Ana whispered.

Tori pressed a button on her hip. There was a flash, and then a photograph slid out from her wrist. "Here you are," she said.

Ana grinned. "Thank you!"

Ifan picked up the necklace made of jade beads and feathers. "I wonder how much this is worth?"

"It's not yours," said Tori firmly. "You know the time-traveller rules – exploring history is fine, but we must never take from it."

"I know," Ifan sighed. "This thing is just so cool."

"Hey!" said Ana. "I've found another door. It's stuck, though."

"I shall open it," said Tori. With robotic strength, she pushed the stone door open. The children stared into the thick gloom of a stone passage.

Suddenly, there was a low, rumbling sound from somewhere above them. Tori stepped out into the passage to investigate.

The next moment, a boulder dropped down from above and bounced off her head. With an electronic squawk, she fell with a crash.

"Tori!" yelled Ana.

The boulder hit the ground and rolled inside the tomb. Rocco, Ana and Ifan dodged past it and ran out to Tori.

"Boulder was … a trap … for tomb robbers," Tori said slowly. "I can self-repair … but it will take time …" Her glowing eyes flickered out.

The rolling boulder struck the stone block where the skeleton lay and the door to the tomb swung shut.

"Oh, no!" said Ana. "There's no handle. We can't get back to the time pod."

"And Tori has conked out," said Rocco. "We're stuck in the past – all alone!"

2 Temple of fear

"We can't just sit here," said Ifan. "We must find a way to get that door open again."

Rocco peered through the gloom. The only light came from tiny cracks in the stone roof overhead. "Let's explore. Maybe there's another way into the tomb."

"What about Tori?" said Ifan.

"Let's carry her," said Ana. "She'll be all right when she's self-repaired."

"We hope," Rocco muttered.

Carrying the robot between them, they slowly moved along a maze of passageways. Colourful murals had been painted on the walls. The statues of strange figures loomed like guards reaching to grab them.

"What if we meet someone?" said Ifan. "We'd better use our wonder-onesies."

Rocco nodded. "Wonder-onesie, dress me as a boy from around here," he said. Suddenly, he was wearing a cotton tunic and a cloak, with deerskin sandals on his feet. "Cool."

"Dress me like him," Ifan said, and the wonder-onesie did as he asked.

"Wonder-onesie, dress me as a girl from this city," said Ana. Next moment, she was wearing a loose yellow blouse and skirt embroidered with bright patterns. The skirt even had a pocket to hold Tori's photo of the tomb. "Not bad!" Ana decided.

"It's a shame we can't disguise Tori," said Ifan. "Maybe we should leave her here."

"She wouldn't leave us, so we won't leave her," said Ana. "Come on, let's see what's up ahead."

They walked on and found an archway in the wall on their right. Steps led down from it into a large, square room. Shafts of sunlight shone in through holes in the roof. The walls were decorated with strange figures on weird thrones. A fire burned behind a large, stone altar.

"It's a temple," Ana realised. "I remember reading that people like the Mayans, the Incas and the Aztecs believed in lots of different gods."

"It stinks in here," said Ifan. He pointed to a doorway across the smoky room. "Come on, let's go."

But as they tiptoed down the steps with Tori, a stocky man came into sight through the doorway. His stern face was pierced with jewellery in his nose, ears and chin. His long, sloping forehead was topped with a headdress made from feathers. Two men with spears followed behind him.

Ana, Rocco and Ifan quickly put down Tori and stood in front of her.

"Intruders!" hissed the man. "I am the high priest of this temple. No one may trespass here."

Ana blinked. She was hearing the high priest's words in English; Tori's voice-to-brain translation was working even if Tori wasn't right now! But would the man understand her, too?

"We didn't mean to," said Ana. "We came from the tomb."

"Liar!" cried the high priest – he understood her even if he didn't believe her. "You will all be punished."

"Wait!" said Ana. "We're not lying! Look!"

She pulled out the photo of the tomb. "This proves we were in there."

The high priest stared at the photograph. "The picture is so real. This ... is magic!"

Just then, Tori bleeped and her eyes glowed weakly into life. "Batteries ... low ..."

"MAGIC!" wailed the high priest. He fell to his knees and so did his warriors. "See! The silver woman's skin shines like a mirror and the girl holds magic paper."

"Yep, we're all magic," said Rocco quickly. "But we mean you no harm."

The high priest gazed at him. "Are you messengers from the world beyond?"

Ana shrugged. "Something like that."

"I must tell King Tlac of your arrival," said the high priest. "Warriors – guard the temple entrance. Let no one enter until I return!"

With that, the high priest ran from the room, followed by his warriors.

Ana turned around to Tori. "Are you okay now?"

"Self-repair is complete, but I need time to recharge," Tori said in a buzzing whisper. "You must get tools ... so we can fix ... the time ... pod."

With that, she fell silent once more.

"Let's see if we can find any," said Rocco.

The children searched the smoky chamber and the passages around it from top to bottom.

"It's no use," said Ana. "There are only statues and cups and things."

The high priest soon returned. "Messengers from the world beyond," he cried. "King Tlac wishes to see you at once."

"The king!" hissed Rocco. "If anyone can get us some tools, he can!"

"Of course!" Ana smiled at the high priest. "It just so happens we want to see the king, too."

The high priest looked at Tori with fearful eyes. "Will she come?"

"Um, no. Tori will rest here in your temple," said Rocco.

"Now, lead the way!" boomed Ifan.

The high priest walked quickly from the room, and the children followed him.

3 The king

The exit from the temple was at the top of a pyramid with steps cut into it. The day was hot and bright. Looking around, Rocco was staggered by how massive the city was. It was built in a grid around wide walkways and a winding river. There were apartment blocks and storehouses, palaces and markets, squares and monuments. Two more pyramids towered like mountains in the distance.

The city was a riot of brilliant colour and teeming with life. Fountains spattered in square pools. The smell of tortillas and spice filled the air. Dazzling designs in paint and jade decorated store fronts and houses. Crowds of people went loudly about their business. Teotihuacan seemed just as busy as the cities in Rocco's own time.

Rocco remembered what Tori had said about the mystery surrounding Teotihuacan: no one knew who had lived here, only that one day it was attacked and everyone left. It was weird to think that a place so busy with life would end so sadly.

I hope we're not still here when it does! Rocco thought.

The children followed the high priest through a gateway into a large and peaceful garden. Inside was a grand building, tiled with jade and decorated with glittering mosaics. A staircase, guarded by warriors, stretched to a doorway.

A small figure came out and stood at the top of the steps. It was a boy of about Ana's age wearing a dark tunic and a headdress of exotic feathers.

"Visitors from beyond!" he called. "I, King Tlac, welcome you to my great city."

Ifan couldn't hide his surprise. "The king is just a boy!"

"His father ruled us but died when Tlac was an infant," said the high priest. "But you know this, of course, since you come from his tomb."

"Um, yeah," said Rocco. "Of course."

"Do magical creatures need to eat and drink?" Tlac called down.

"Yes, we do," replied Ana, her stomach growling at the thought of a meal.

"Then please join me for food and drink in my throne room. Let us talk together."

The high priest led the way up the steps and presented the children to Tlac. Ana bowed, and Rocco and Ifan did the same. The king beamed at his strange visitors and learned their names.

Tlac led them into his throne room. It was large and cool, with red walls covered in beautiful paintings. The floor was strewn with petals. Tlac sat down on a magnificent throne of wood and jade.

"My priest says you have a picture that looks like real life," said the king.

"We call it a photograph," said Ana, and she gave him the picture of the tomb. "Here. Keep it."

"Truly, you possess great magic," said King Tlac. He placed the photo beside his throne. "Thank you. What can I give you in return?"

"Tools!" said Rocco. "We'd like to see all the different tools you have."

"Really? That's a boring way to thank you," said Tlac. "I know! You can be my royal guests at the sports tournament tomorrow! The first game is kick-ball, and I myself am playing."

"Is that like football?" said Ifan. "I'd love to play a real game. I've only ever played virtual football in my bedroom ..."

"Your words are strange, boy of magic. But if you wish to play kick-ball against me, then so you shall!" Tlac clapped his hands. "High priest! Please escort our guests back to the temple ... and arrange for one each of every tool in the city to be brought to them."

The high priest bowed and said, "It shall be done."

* * *

Ana, Rocco and Ifan were taken back to the temple. As soon as the high priest left them, they told Tori what had happened.

"Well done, all of you," said Tori. "My power is still low after my self-repair. But when I am fully charged, I will use robotic strength to get back inside the tomb and reach the time pod. I only hope those cracked fuel rods don't explode before I can mend them."

"Me, too," said Ana.

"I'm glad we've got the sports tournament tomorrow to take our mind off things," said Ifan. "I can't wait to play!"

Dozens of strange tools arrived through the afternoon and evening – stone knives for cutting, shark teeth for piercing ears, flat wooden swords, copper needles and many others.

Rocco picked up a wooden axe. "Good luck repairing the time pod with this stuff!"

"What about that drive unit thingy we pulled out of the wreck," said Ana. "You know, Tori, the one we crashed into. Might that be useful for spare parts or something?"

"Good idea, Ana." Tori pulled the squashed black box with its red wires from her pocket and picked up one of the copper needles. "I'll get it open and look inside. In the meantime, you children should recharge in your own way – by sleeping."

"I guess I should rest." Ifan yawned. "I really want to thrash King Tlac at kick-ball tomorrow!"

Rocco didn't sleep well on the stone floor – mostly because of Tori. Being a robot, she didn't need to sleep – and she spent the whole night humming tunelessly while she worked.

The morning sun had barely risen outside when the high priest swept into the temple. "Rocco, boy of magic!" he said. "I hope you were pleased with our tools."

"Um ... yeah." Rocco yawned. "They were awesome. Thanks."

"In exchange, the king has a favour to ask." The high priest smiled and bowed. "Please, will you join me outside?"

Ana opened one eye. "Want me to come with you?"

Rocco got up slowly, aching from his night on the stone floor. "I don't need my little sister to babysit me, thanks!"

Outside, the high priest was waiting with six men.

"Since you and the king are similar heights and ages, he asks that you wear his royal crown and take his place on a trip in the royal canoe."

"How come?" said Rocco. "Is he having a lie-in?"

"On the first day of each sports tournament, King Tlac has a tradition," the high priest explained. "He carries the kick-ball into the forest and places it beneath the tallest tree. In this way, he gains the speed and stamina of the strongest animals in the forest."

"Fair enough," said Rocco. "How come he wants to send me in his place?"

The high priest smiled. "Because today, the king wants to practise kick-ball in secret. He fears your magical friend, Ifan, will be impossible to beat."

Rocco smiled too. "Well, the royal canoe sounds pretty cool, so I'm happy to help. I'll just tell my friends."

The high priest bowed. "Of course."

Rocco quickly filled in Ana, Tori and Ifan about his royal mission.

Ifan grinned. "So, I've got Tlac worried. Nice!"

"Not as nice as a royal boat trip," said Ana. "Wish I could come."

"Sorry." Rocco winked at her. "As king, I can't allow that."

He left the temple and walked off with the king's guards through the quiet city streets to where the royal canoe bobbed on the river. The craft was carved from mighty trees. It was as long as a bus but only half as wide.

Rocco sat on a wooden throne covered with cushions. Beside him was a rubber ball the size of a bowling ball. People lined the sides of the river to salute him. Keeping his face hidden by the headdress, Rocco waved back as the guards started to row. *I could get used to the life of a king!* he thought.

The guards used their paddles well, propelling the canoe along the glittering water. Soon, they had left the city behind. The riverbanks were thick with trees and bushes. No one was about.

Then a voice shouted from the undergrowth:
"Aha! There is King Tlac, on his way to bless his
silly ball."

Rocco frowned. "Huh?"

Ten fierce-looking warriors rose up from the
bushes waving spears. Their leader stepped
forward and pointed at Rocco. "GET HIM!"

4 Double danger

The warriors attacked! *WHOOSH!* A spear flew over Rocco's head.

"It is an ambush!" cried the guard beside him. "Get paddling!"

Rocco ducked down. "Who are these guys?"

"Enemies of King Tlac," said the guard beside him. "Quickly, use your magic powers against them."

Rocco groaned. "That might be tricky," he said. He ducked as another spear shot by, lost his balance – and toppled into the water! The cold water was like a slap to Rocco's whole body. He struggled back to the surface – only for enemy warriors to grab him and haul him out of the water. The others went on hurling spears at the king's canoe.

"There are too many to fight!" cried the chief guard as the canoe turned and quickly powered back towards the city. "We shall return with more guards!"

"Great," Rocco yelled back. "What am I meant to do in the meantime?"

Just then, a large, scowling man emerged from the trees. "Good work, my warriors!" he snarled. "I, King Itza, have captured the ruler of Teotihuacan!"

"You haven't," Rocco gasped. "I'm just a normal kid."

"Nice try, Tlac!" King Itza laughed. "You were travelling in the royal canoe. You wear the royal headdress."

Wear! thought Rocco. *I've got my wonder-onesie on. I can change outfits and give these guys a big surprise!* He cleared his throat. "Wonder-onesie – dress me as a knight in shining armour!"

But his cloak only gave a damp splutter, and nothing happened.

Rocco groaned. "I guess wonder-onesies aren't waterproof!"

"Stop this babbling," said King Itza. "I will lead you through my city in chains, Tlac. Then, if you want to stay alive, you will give control of Teotihuacan to ME!"

"I already told you, I'm not King Tlac!" cried Rocco.

* * *

Back at the temple, Ana and Ifan ate fruit outside while Tori continued fiddling with the old drive unit they'd crashed into.

"Lucky Rocco, getting to ride in the king's canoe," said Ana. "I bet he's loving it!"

Before Ifan could reply, King Tlac swept up to the temple. He was short of breath, like he'd been exercising. "Greetings, children of magic!"

"Er, hello," she said. "I thought you would be hiding away while Rocco is out pretending to be you."

"Rocco and my guards are late coming back," said Tlac.

Ana felt her heart jump. "How come? What's happened?"

"You are magic – can't you tell me?" King Tlac shrugged. "I am sure they will be here soon. In the meantime, Ana, I come to give you a great honour. I would like you to open our sporting tournament."

Ana blinked. "Me?"

"Who better," said Tlac, "since your magical friend, Ifan, will be playing against me in the first game in front of thousands of people?"

"Thousands?" cried Ifan. "I thought you meant we'd be having a kickabout with maybe 20 people watching. Not in a big stadium!"

"When I take part in the games, everyone watches!" said Tlac proudly. "And remember, there is wealth and glory for the winning side ... but the losers will be fed to the crocodiles!"

"What?" Ana and Ifan cried together.

"Still, you have nothing to fear, eh, Ifan? Your magic will keep you safe!" Tlac grinned.

"Um, hold on a second, Great King," said Ana. "I want to ask Tori if she'll go with us."

"Sorry, I can't." Tori stood at the top of the temple steps, and Ana and Ifan ran up to join her. "I must finish my repairs."

"What about me?" said Ifan. "No one can repair me if I get eaten by crocodiles!"

"I am sure you will play well against Tlac," said Tori. "But I will switch my satellite dish to 'distress mode' – if you need me, I will race to you."

"Well, okay," said Ana. "Keep listening!"

She and Ifan returned to King Tlac, who strode away. Ifan wasn't happy.

"I can't even use my wonder-onesie to protect me," he groaned. "Crocs live in rivers, and smart-clothes don't work well in water."

"Just concentrate on playing a good game," Ana said. "If you lose, we'll think of something ..."

* * *

Meanwhile, Rocco was being marched through the tropical forest by King Itza and his warriors. He knew that every step he took was leading him further from safety. Not only that, but thorns were scratching his bare legs as he walked.

Suddenly, he heard a quiet, digital *BONG!* It was a sound he had heard before ...

My wonder-onesie, Rocco thought. *It must have dried out!* In a flash of light, he was wearing a suit of armour – just what he'd asked for back in the river!

The warriors screamed. "King Tlac has become a monster!" cried one.

Rocco swung around, hardly able to see through his helmet. He saw King Itza with a wooden club. "I do not fear your magic, boy!" he said, and brought down the club. *CLANG!* It bounced off Rocco's metal helmet.

"RUN, ITZA!" boomed Rocco in his spookiest voice. "OR ELSE!"

Itza turned and fled. "I will be back, Tlac!" he shouted. "I will conquer your city!"

"Yeah?" called Rocco. "You and whose army?"

"Me and MY army!" Itza replied, and crashed away through the bushes.

"Hmmm. I don't like the sound of that." Rocco remembered what Tori had said when they'd first arrived, about how the city came to an end: "It was attacked and left deserted at the end of the sixth century ..."

Would Teotihuacan be attacked by Itza and his army?

Rocco turned and stumbled away in the opposite direction. He crashed past branches and pushed through bushes. The armour was super-heavy, but he knew that each time you asked the wonder-onesie to change, you wore down its power. He didn't want to be stuck in his tunic and sandals if Itza's warriors came after him again.

But very soon, his heart began to sink. Rocco had no idea where he was or which way to go.

He was lost!

5 Disaster!

While Rocco was lost and alone in the forest, Ana found herself stuck in the stadium. Huge numbers of sweaty, unwashed people were all squashed inside, standing on stone platforms overlooking the ball court, cheering and shouting. She sat in a small, stone tower with the high priest – the finest seats in the stadium with the best view of the action.

Ana looked out over the ball court. It was hemmed in by walls, like an enormous pit, smooth with cement and shaped like a long capital I. Stone rings were placed high up on the painted walls. Ana supposed they were goals for the ball to pass through.

"Hear me!" cried the high priest, rising to his feet. The crowd fell silent.

"We have a special observer today!" he went on. "A friend to King Tlac from the world beyond, with powers of magic. Welcome, Ana!"

Blushing, Ana stood up and the crowd went wild with applause and cheering. She felt like a pop star!

The high priest raised his hands for quiet. "Today King Tlac will play against another mystical visitor – Ifan!"

King Tlac marched out on to the court, wearing deerskin pads on his hips and elbows. Ifan trailed behind him, dressed the same. Yells and cheers rang out as the boy king greeted his people. Ifan gave a weak little wave. Another man came out on to the court. The referee, thought Ana. He held a dark rubber ball, the size of a child's football. It rattled as it bounced.

"What's inside the ball?" Ana asked.

"A human skull!" The high priest smiled. "We wrap the rubber around it, so the ball weighs less and travels further."

"I wish I hadn't asked," Ana muttered.

"The special contest today is one on one!" the referee announced. "The ball must stay in play at all times and not touch the ground. You may hit the ball with your hip, leg, foot, shoulder or head. A goal is worth two points. First to score 20 points is the winner. The loser is thrown to the crocodiles."

"Let us play!" boomed Tlac, and the stadium burst into excited applause.

The referee threw the ball to the king, who booted it to Ifan.

Ifan tried to head it – and yelped as the ball whacked his nose. The ball hit the ground and the crowd gasped.

"Penalty!" shouted the referee. "One point to King Tlac!"

Tlac raised his fist and the audience cheered.

"Play again!" the referee called.

This time, Ifan kicked the ball at the wall. It bounced off and Tlac skilfully trapped the ball with his shoulder and let it drop to his knee. Then he flicked the ball in the air and kicked it with his left foot. The ball sailed through one of the stone hoops and the crowd went crazy once more.

"Two points to King Tlac!" said the referee.

"That means he's got three points altogether," Ana muttered. "Come on, Ifan!"

It was King Tlac's turn to start play. He kicked the ball so hard it bounced first off one wall, then the other. But Ifan got to it and kicked it at a hoop. He missed the hole and the ball bounced back at him. He sent it over Tlac's head and the ball hit the ground before the king could reach it.

"One point to Ifan!" called the referee.

"Well played, Ifan," said Tlac.

Ifan said nothing. He was already panting for breath. Ana guessed Ifan's workouts at home were not in the blazing hot sunshine.

WHAP! King Tlac kicked the ball along the court. Ifan dived, trying to get his head to it – but was a second too slow.

"4–1 to King Tlac!" called the referee over the roaring of the crowd.

"This looks like it will be a short game," the high priest observed. "I look forward to seeing your friend use his magic to escape the crocodiles."

Ana shuddered. *Tori, I hope you're listening out for anyone in trouble – I think we'll need your help!*

* * *

Back in the jungle, Rocco was lost, hot and very, very worried. Then he heard someone crashing through the undergrowth. Someone getting closer and closer …

A familiar figure came barging out of the bushes.

"Tori!" Rocco gave her a relieved hug. "I'm so glad you're here!"

"Ana asked me to switch my satellite dish to 'distress mode'. I sensed you were in trouble, so I came straight here," Tori said. "But Ifan needs help, too. We must hurry back to the city. You'd better get out of that armour."

"Wonder-onesie, dress me like a boy from around here," Rocco said. Slowly, the heavy armour was replaced by shorts and sandals. "What's up with Ifan?"

"He is playing kick-ball against King Tlac in the arena. If he loses, he'll be thrown to the crocodiles. Come on!"

Back in the stadium, Ana was biting her nails. Ifan was playing as well as he could, but Tlac was ahead 19 points to 11.

If Tlac got one more point, he would win!

"Prepare for defeat, Ifan!" Tlac laughed as he kicked the ball.

There was a sudden *BOOM* and a massive explosion rocked the stadium. People were scattered like skittles. Ifan and the king were thrown to the ground. A huge column of smoke rose up in the distance – coming from the temple pyramid. Even from where Ana was, she could see that half the temple had been blown away.

"The tomb has burst open!" wailed the high priest. "Why?"

Ana's heart sank down to her sandals. "I have a horrid feeling it's because of us!"

6 Surprise attack

Rocco and Tori were running through the fields just outside the city when the explosion went off. The blast threw them both to the shaking ground.

Rocco raised his head. "What was that?"

"There is only one thing here that could make such an explosion," said Tori. "The time pod!" Her satellite dish whizzed about like a food mixer. "The fuel rods have blown up. I was afraid they would."

"But that means we're stuck here in sixth-century Mexico," breathed Rocco. "For ever!"

"It's worse than that," said Tori. "Look!" She gestured at the plants around them. They were starting to wither and rot. The soil was turning red. Within minutes, all the plants were gone.

"Everything's dying!" said Rocco. "Why?"

"The exploding fuel rods contain special radiation," Tori explained. "It doesn't hurt people, but it will poison the land and the river," Tori said sadly. "Without food and water, no one will be able to live here."

Rocco gasped. "Tori, you said when we arrived that no one knew why the people moved out of this city and left it empty. It must be because of those fuel rods. It's all our fault!"

King Tlac's chief guard burst into the field, followed by warriors. "Rocco, we have been looking for you," he said. He stared at Tori. "Did your magic friend help you to get away?"

"Something like that," said Rocco. "Come on. We must find King Tlac. There's lots we must tell him!"

After the explosion, the stadium was hushed. Ana ran down to the ball court on wobbly legs while the rest of the crowd stared around in fear.

"High priest!" Tlac shouted. "What has happened?"

"Perhaps the gods are angry with us!" cried the high priest.

"No!" came a squeaky, metal voice. "It is just a terrible accident." Gasps of awe and wonder came from the crowd as Tori strode into the stadium, her silver skin dazzling in the sun.

"It is the fourth of our visitors!" cooed the high priest.

"Truly, she is the most magical of all!" said the king.

"Listen to me, all of you," Tori called. "This city has been ... er, hit by a kind of magic thunderbolt. I am sorry but you must move away. The crops have died and the water has turned bad. To stay here means certain doom!"

Everyone gasped and turned to Tlac. The boy king stood there in shock.

Then Ana saw Rocco come in behind Tori with a bunch of guards. Rocco ran up to her. "Are you okay?" he said.

"No!" Ana whispered, feeling awful. "Everyone here has lost their home, thanks to us."

"It's not our fault we crashed into that old drive unit," Ifan said. "We didn't mean to come here."

King Tlac spoke at last. "Where can we go?"

"I believe you are friends with other rulers," said Tori. "They will help you."

"Excuse me, my king!" said the chief guard.

"King Itza tried to capture you. He took the magic boy, Rocco, instead."

"But I got away," Rocco said quickly.

"How dare Itza attack me!" Tlac frowned. "If we must leave Teotihuacan, perhaps we can take his city? Or build a better one." He smiled at the crowd. "Whatever we do, my friends, remember this – a city is not only made of stone. It is made of people. If we stay together, we can do anything, anywhere!"

* * *

The sports tournament came to an early end, much to Ifan's relief. He, Rocco and Ana spent the rest of the day helping people pack up their things. Meanwhile, Tori scanned the land and water all around and told people where it was safe to eat and drink.

By the next morning, most people had already left the city. Many went in canoes. Some went on foot, carrying their belongings on their backs.

Ana, Rocco, Ifan and Tori stood in the remains of the tomb. The explosion had wrecked the whole temple. The time pod was now just a twisted metal wreck.

"Looks like we're stuck here," said Rocco.

Ifan nodded, bouncing one of the rubber balls from the stadium. "At least there's a whole lot of space here. And plenty of time to improve my game!"

Tlac and the high priest approached them.

"A new adventure is about to begin for the people of this city," Tlac said.

"That's a nice way to look at it," said Ana.

Tlac shrugged. "My father left this place. Now I must leave it, too."

"Your father rose to greatness to rule this city," said the high priest. "Now, you have a chance to prove that you will be an even greater king."

"And I *shall* prove it," Tlac said. He smiled at Tori and the children. "Perhaps we will meet again one day."

"I hope so," said Ana. She and the other three bowed as the boy king and his high priest left to join their people.

Tori pulled the little black box with the red wires from her pocket. "I have finished work on this drive unit."

"Crashing into that left us stranded here," said Rocco. "What good is it to us now?"

"It is the drive unit of a time machine," Tori reminded them, placing the box beside the time pod. "It can push things forward through time or send them backwards."

"So can that help us?" Ana asked.

"I hope so. I have tried to boost its energy." Tori crossed her robotic fingers. "With any luck, it will put time into reverse – but only for the pod."

"Ha! Like rewinding history!" Ifan beamed. "That will undo all the damage – the time pod will be as good as new."

"It sounds impossible and crazy to me," said Rocco. "But if it works, who cares!"

"It will take a lot of power," said Tori, switching on the drive unit. "Here goes!"

Suddenly, Ana heard something from outside – a wild chanting and cheering coming from the forests still standing beyond the barren soil. "What's that?" she asked.

Ana peered over the broken temple wall and saw hundreds of fierce warriors creeping out from the poisoned trees. Some held spears. Some held flaming torches. They were led by an angry-looking man in a huge headdress.

"Uh-oh," said Rocco. "That's King Itza, the guy who tried to get me."

"Can you hear me, Tlac?" yelled King Itza. "I have come to take your city by force. The people of Teotihuacan shall serve me, not you!"

"Except there aren't any people left!" said Ifan.

Ana gasped. "Just think – if everyone was still here in the city, there would be a terrible battle. Thousands of people would die!"

"Maybe the time pod crashing here wasn't just an unlucky accident," said Rocco. "It actually saved lives!"

"That makes me feel better," said Ifan. "But King Itza won't be happy when he finds out that we're the only ones still here!"

"Tori," said Ana, worried. "How long will it take to fix the time pod?"

"I don't know," said Tori. "The time power is still building."

"Then we're in big trouble," Rocco groaned. "Itza's going to march straight in here and get us."

"Maybe we can distract him." Ifan bounced the rubber ball on the ground and smiled. "Let's see if I can put this to good use ..."

Ana held her breath as Ifan sized up the shot and kicked the ball. *THWACK!* The ball flew through the air ... and hit King Itza right on the head!

"OW!" Itza cried out and fell backwards. His warriors gasped and followed him into the bushes, fearing a full-on attack.

"Brilliant shot, Ifan!" said Rocco.

"Thanks," said Ifan. "But I don't think they'll be gone for long."

"Maybe we won't need very long!" Ana pointed to the wreck of the time pod, which was glowing and sparking. "Tori, it looks like it's working."

"Yes!" Tori squeaked. "Yes, I think it is!"

Thick, dark smoke started sucking into the wreck, like a film played backwards. Bits of metal unbent themselves. The windows unshattered. Levers and switches grew like mushrooms from the control panel.

Ifan jumped for joy. "The time pod is rewinding!"

Unfortunately, as he jumped, he was spotted – by King Itza.

"You shall pay for that cowardly attack, boy!" Itza snarled, rubbing his head. "Warriors – charge!"

Itza's warriors poured out from the forest, shouting battle cries.

Finally, with a blast of light, the time pod was back to normal.

"Everyone in!" Tori shrieked, snatching up the drive unit from the ground.

Ana, Rocco and Ifan dived inside – just as King Itza climbed over the ruins of the wall. "What is happening?" he snarled.

"This time tour is departing now," said Tori politely. "Goodbye!"

She shot into the time pod and the door slid closed behind her.

"Noooooo!" raged King Itza. "Warriors – attack that strange chariot!"

Spears and clubs began battering the windows.

"Get us out of here, Tori!" shouted Ifan.

Tori was already working the controls. "There's no time to set a course," she said. "We'll have to do an emergency take-off and see where we end up."

Rocco grinned at Ana. "I hope it's somewhere quiet and safe!"

"Fat chance!" said Ana, smiling back.

Covers came down over the windows and the time pod spun up into the air ...

Then, a moment later, it vanished.

The four friends were flying off again – to who knew where!

Chat about the book

1 Read Chapter 1. Where did the time pod make an emergency landing?

2 Read page 14. Why did Tori speak firmly to Ifan?

3 Go to page 23. What word tells you that Rocco was surprised by the size of the city?

4 Read page 21. Why do you think Rocco said, "Yep, we're all magic"?

5 Go to page 37. Why did Ana's heart jump?

6 Read page 12. How did Ifan and Ana react to what they saw when Tori switched on the torch?

7 'The time pod shot away like a rollercoaster.' Why do you think the author described the time pod like this?

8 Would you like to take a Time Tours holiday? Give reasons for and against.